CANOEING

is for me

CANOEING
is for me

Tom Moran

photographs by
Robert L. Wolfe

 Lerner Publications Company   Minneapolis

The author wishes to thank the Southern California Canoe Association for its help with this book.

LIBRARY OF CONGRESS CATALOGING IN PUBLICATION DATA

Moran, Tom.
  Canoeing is for me.

  Summary: Two brothers describe basic canoeing skills; then take a day-long trip during which they practice these skills.
  1. Canoes and canoeing—Juvenile literature.
[1. Canoes and canoeing] I. Wolfe, Robert L., ill.
II. Title.
GV783.M67   1983   797.1'22   83-19957
  ISBN 0-8225-1142-8 (lib. bdg.)

Manufactured in the United States of America

International Standard Book Number: 0-8225-1142-8
Library of Congress Catalog Number: 83-19957

1 2 3 4 5 6 7 8 9 10 93 92 91 90 89 88 87 86 85 84

Hi! My name is Adam, and this is my brother, John Paul. We learned how to canoe this summer. It's very easy to learn how to paddle a canoe, and you can go many places in a canoe that you can't reach any other way. Canoeing is an exciting sport, and it's lots of fun, too. Let me tell you some of the things I've learned about canoeing.

Canoes are long, narrow boats. The front and back of a canoe look almost exactly the same. That is why a canoe is called a **double-ended** boat. Because of their shape, canoes are able to speed easily through the water.

Canoes were very important in the exploration and early history of North America. The North American Indians built and used canoes covered with animal hides and birch bark. The canoes that we use today are very similar to the Indian and explorer boats of long ago.

Canoes have many uses. They can be paddled on lakes, rivers, and the ocean. Many people like to take their canoes on long camping trips into the wilderness. A canoe can carry a heavy load of camping gear, food, and other supplies. And canoeing is a great way to enjoy nature. It's very peaceful and quiet paddling a canoe near a woodsy shore.

Modern canoes are much stronger and lighter than the old Indian skin-and-wood boats. Many different canoe models and styles are available today. Canoes are made from wood, fiberglass, metal, or various types of plastics. Most modern canoes are durable and easy to repair.

The canoe that we usually use is made of aluminum, a strong and lightweight metal. It's 15 feet long and designed for recreational use by young paddlers like us. Boats like this are easy to handle, so we can take them many different places.

STERN

THWARTS

GUNWALE

BOW

The front end of a canoe is called the **bow**. The other end is called the **stern**. The top edges of the boat's sides are called the **gunwales** (GUN-uhls). Some canoes have a **keel**. A keel is a raised strip in the center of the canoe's bottom surface. A keel helps a canoe move forward through the water in a straight line.

KEEL

The horizontal bars bridging between the gunwales of a canoe are called **thwarts**. They give the boat added strength and can be leaned against while paddling.

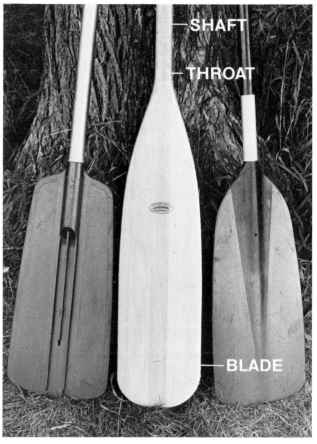

Canoe paddles are made from many different materials including wood, plastic, and fiberglass. We often use paddles made of aluminum and plastic. The flat part of the paddle is called the **blade**. The blade is the part that moves through the water. It's connected to a long, thin section called the **shaft**. The blade and shaft are joined at the **throat**.

The **grip** is the part that you hold onto while paddling. It is located on the shaft at the opposite end from the blade. Some grips are rounded and pear shaped. Other paddles have a **T-grip**. This grip gives me good paddling control.

PEAR-SHAPED GRIP

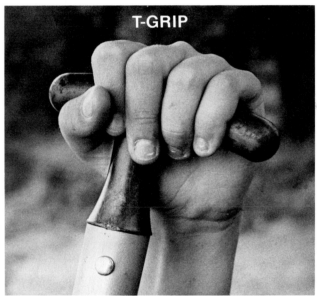
T-GRIP

There are lots of places to learn how to canoe. John Paul and I learned by taking a course at a lake near our home. We learned canoeing safety, proper paddling, and other skills. Safety is very important in canoeing. You must be a good swimmer before you canoe. If you had an accident, you might have to swim to shore or stay afloat until help arrived.

We *always* wear life jackets when we canoe. They are called **personal flotation devices** or **PFDs.** The jackets are comfortable and do not interfere with paddling movements. They help keep you afloat if your boat tips over or if you fall out of the canoe. There are several kinds of PFDs to choose from.

One of the first things John Paul and I learned in our class was how to get into a canoe and launch it safely. Empty canoes seem stable, but it is very easy to tip them over if you are not careful getting into them! You must keep your weight balanced near the center of the boat or the canoe will roll over and throw you into the water.

Entering a canoe from a small pier is easy when done correctly. The bow paddler gets in first, and the stern paddler is the last to go aboard. When I am going to paddle in the stern, I hold the canoe close to the dock while John Paul and any other passengers climb into it. Then John Paul grabs onto the canoe's gunwales and steadies himself as he climbs aboard and takes his position in the bow. He then holds the canoe against the pier as I enter it in the stern.

We can launch a canoe from shore, too. The boat is pushed into the water so that the bow points directly away from shore. The bow paddler gets in first. John Paul climbs aboard and walks slowly to his position while I hold the boat steady. Then I climb in, move toward him, and shift my weight until the boat begins to float. John Paul paddles toward deeper water as I carefully return to my position in the stern.

John Paul and I usually paddle sitting down. But many canoeists prefer to kneel in their canoes. Kneeling keeps the boat's **center of gravity**, an imaginary balance point, much lower than if you sit on the seats. A low center of gravity helps make the canoe more stable.

Some paddlers kneel on only one knee. Others use both knees.

John Paul and I had learned many different paddle strokes at our lessons. Each one has a special purpose. Many seemed awkward at first, but they became easy with practice.

The basic paddling technique is called the **forward stroke**. Sometimes it's called the **power, straight,** or **bow stroke**. It is a very natural motion and is easy to learn.

I hold the grip with one hand and grasp the shaft several inches above the throat with my other hand. Then I swing the paddle forward, keeping the blade nearly parallel to the water's surface. This is called **feathering.** When my shaft hand is fully extended, I lift the grip slightly and the blade drops into the water. This is called the **catch**.

I then push the grip forward and pull back on the shaft with my other hand. The blade moves backward through the water and propels the canoe forward. When the blade comes out of the water, it is in position to repeat the stroke sequence.

The forward stroke is done in a smooth, continuous motion. It can be used for a long time without tiring out the paddler.

When John Paul and I canoe together, we paddle on opposite sides of the boat. When we trade sides, our grip and shaft hands reverse position. When we paddle together and both use the forward stroke, the canoe moves in a straight line.

BACK STROKE

The **back stroke** is almost the exact opposite of the forward stroke. You pull on the paddle grip while pushing forward with the shaft hand. This stroke is used to slow down or back up a canoe. It is very useful in rivers or when coming toward a dock or the shore. The back stroke is sometimes called the **backwater stroke**.

Another basic stroke is called the **draw stroke**. To do the draw, reach out over the gunwale and dip the blade into the water as far from the boat as you can easily reach. Then pull the blade toward the boat. The draw stroke moves the canoe toward the paddling side.

The **push stroke,** or **pushover,** is the opposite of the draw stroke. To start a push stroke, put the paddle in the water very close to the side of the canoe. Keep the blade parallel with the canoe's gunwales and push it away from the side of the boat. This will move the boat sideways, pushing it away from the side on which you are paddling.

PUSH STROKE

If I use a draw stroke on my side, and John Paul uses a push stroke on the opposite side, the canoe will move toward my side. This is an excellent way to keep away from rocks and other hazards without having to change paddling sides. All of these strokes can be used to move the canoe quickly and firmly sideways.

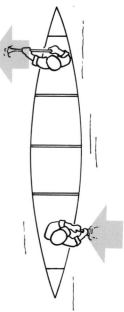

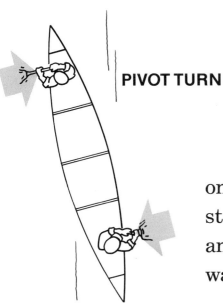

PIVOT TURN

When John Paul and I use draw strokes on opposite sides of the canoe, the boat starts to turn. This is called the **pivot turn**, and it is a good stroke to use when you want to head in a different direction.

Turning is also easy with the **sweep stroke.** To make a sweep stroke, I extend my paddle forward and then pull the blade back through the water in a long arc. This motion swings the canoe's bow away from the side where the paddling is done. This is sometimes called the **C-stroke.**

A **reverse sweep** is very similar to the C-stroke. It is started with the paddle behind you. You dip it into the water and push it forward and outward in a wide, sweeping arc. This stroke will turn the canoe's bow toward the paddling side.

A canoe can be turned very quickly using shortened sweep strokes. The bow paddler makes a forward sweep stroke, while the stern paddler uses a reverse sweep on the opposite side. The canoe turns in a complete circle.

We also learned an important steering stroke. It is called the **J-stroke** and is very helpful when you are canoeing alone. When you are paddling by yourself, your canoe will naturally veer away from the side on which you are paddling. With a steering stroke like the J-stroke, you paddle on just one side while controlling the canoe and staying on a straight course.

J-STROKE

The J-stroke starts just like the forward stroke. But halfway through the stroke, you push the paddle blade outward and away from the boat at an angle. This forces the boat back on course without slowing it too much.

The blade moves through the water in the shape of the letter *J*. The stern paddler in a two-person boat can also use a J-stroke to correct the boat's course when necessary.

There are many canoe strokes. We learned the most basic ones. The more strokes a canoeist knows, the easier it is to control the boat.

One day, after John Paul and I had taken several lessons, we went on a day-long canoe trip at Cedar Lake. Our Aunt Diane and cousin Joanne took us. Joanne's friends Mark and Laura came along, too.

When we got to the lake, we had to unload the canoes from the tops of the cars. This is hard work! John Paul and I helped with the ropes, but we just watched as Mark took down the canoes. Mark had to ask another man to help him with this job.

Cedar Lake was very pretty. John Paul and I were excited about practicing all the canoeing strokes we had learned and seeing some beautiful scenery, too. We decided to launch the canoes from a small dock where many canoes were kept.

To get to the dock, we had to carry the canoes through some narrow trails in the woods. Everybody helped. The easiest way to carry a canoe is called the **four-person carry**. Two people hold the boat's bow while the other two carry the stern.

Sometimes you will encounter places where it is necessary to carry your canoe overland until the water conditions improve. This is called **portaging**.

On our way to the lake, the trail became too narrow for us to continue the four-person carry. So we decided that Mark would portage the canoes. Experienced canoeists like Mark usually portage their canoes upside-down on their shoulders. Some canoes are fitted with padded **yokes** to make them easier to carry. You can also make a yoke by tying a set of paddles to the canoe's thwarts.

When we got to the dock, we loaded our gear onto the canoes. Everything had been put into waterproof backpacks. We tried to place the weight of paddlers and gear evenly throughout the canoe so that the boat would be stable and easy to handle. This is called keeping the canoe **trim**. It's a good idea to carry an extra paddle, a life preserver, and rope as safety precautions.

After we put on our PFDs, we launched the boats. John Paul started in the bow position, and I paddled from the stern. The canoes stayed in a line so that we could tell where everyone was at all times. John Paul and I were the lead canoe. Our friends followed behind us.

We kept close to the shore as we paddled along the lake. The wind was blowing lightly and made small waves on the surface of the water. The sharp nose of the canoe moved easily through the waves.

We paddled to the far side of the lake where there were lily pads growing in the water. Tall reeds stuck high out of the lake. John Paul and I almost got lost in them!

While paddling around the lily pads, we saw several frogs and a turtle. John Paul watched for birds with his binoculars. One of the things we love best about canoeing is that you're sure to see animals and birds you don't see from land. And it's so quiet and peaceful on a lake. We just drifted for awhile, enjoying the scenery. Diane, Joanne, Mark, and Laura decided to watch some people who were fishing from another canoe nearby.

We traveled around the lake for a while longer, and soon we were hungry. We stopped for lunch at a clearing on shore. We made sure to pull our canoes well up onto the shore so that they wouldn't float away.

After all that paddling we had worked up big appetites. Lunch tasted great. As we ate, we talked about some of the birds we had seen and looked them up in a bird book.

When it was time to move on, we paddled toward a channel connecting Cedar Lake with another small lake. We passed under an old railroad bridge. It was a little tricky steering the canoes under the bridge, but we used the J-stroke to keep us on course. We passed through a nice park, and some ducks swam up to us.

On the way back through the channel, we stopped at a lemonade stand specially set up for canoeists on the water's edge. The lemonade was just what we needed before heading back to Cedar Lake.

When we reached our starting point, John Paul and I tipped over our canoe on purpose and let it fill up with water. We wanted to practice what to do if this actually happened.

We sat on top of the filled canoe and paddled it back to shore with our arms. We also practiced emptying the canoe by rocking it back and forth. Then I held the bow steady while John Paul reached over the gunwale and gradually worked his way back aboard. He then moved his weight to balance the boat as I crawled inside it.

Aunt Diane told us it was time to go. It had been a great day of canoeing, but we were all very tired. I rested under a tree for a while before we loaded up and left for home.

Our paddling was over for the day, but we knew that there were more lake and river trips awaiting us. John Paul and I were both eager for our next canoe trip. We knew that canoeing was for us!

Words about CANOEING

BACK STROKE: A paddling stroke useful in backing up and slowing down a canoe. Also called the *backwater stroke.*

BLADE: The thin flat portion of a paddle that moves through the water

BOW: The front end of a canoe

CATCH: Part of the stroking motion in which the blade is dropped into the water

CENTER OF GRAVITY: The balance point of a canoe

DRAW STROKE: A paddling stroke used for moving a canoe sideways and for turning

FEATHERING: Keeping the paddle blade parallel to the water surface as it moves through the air

FORWARD STROKE: A basic paddling stroke used for moving forward. Also called the *power, straight,* or *bow* stroke.

GRIP: The end of a paddle that is designed to be held in one hand

GUNWALES: The top edges of a canoe's sides.

J-STROKE: A basic canoe steering stroke

KEEL: A strip along the center of the canoe's bottom surface designed to keep the boat moving straight

PERSONAL FLOTATION DEVICE (PFD): A life jacket or flotation cushion

PIVOT TURN: A method of turning a canoe

POLING: Using a long wooden pole to propel a canoe

PORTAGING: Carrying a canoe overland

PUSH STROKE: A paddling stroke used to move a canoe sideways. Also called the *pushover.*

RAPIDS: Fast-moving and usually rocky river sections

REVERSE SWEEP: A paddling stroke that moves the canoe's bow toward the paddling side

SHAFT: The long thin portion of a paddle

STERN: The rear end of a canoe

SWEEP: A turning stroke in which the paddle blade makes a wide arc in the water. Also called the *C-stroke.*

T-GRIP: A paddle grip shaped like the letter *T*

THROAT: The point where the shaft and blade of a paddle meet

THWARTS: Horizontal bars that bridge across the gunwales to give a canoe added strength

TRIM: The proper loading of passengers and equipment in a canoe

WHITEWATER: River sections with strong rapids and large waves

YOKE: Special pads for carrying a canoe on the shoulders

ABOUT THE AUTHOR

TOM MORAN is the author of two photographic books and several books in the *Sports For Me* series. He has coached youth football, soccer, and boxing, and he frequently writes on sports subjects for California magazines and newspapers. Mr. Moran lives in Venice, California, where he recently restored a pre-1920 Morris canoe to its original condition.

ABOUT THE PHOTOGRAPHER

ROBERT L. WOLFE attended the University of Minnesota where he studied physical therapy, and the Minneapolis College of Art and Design where he studied photography. He was the senior medical photographer at the University of Minnesota for several years and taught bio-medical photography. He now has a freelance photography business in Minneapolis, Minnesota. An avid canoeist, Mr. Wolfe's photos have illustrated several books in the *Sports For Me* series.